To Kate and Lily,
for inspiring us every day.
We love you exactly the way you are.

You are small.

I am not small.
You are big.

They are just like me.
You are small.

I am not small.
See?

They are just like *me*.
You are big.

You are *all* small!

You are *all* big!

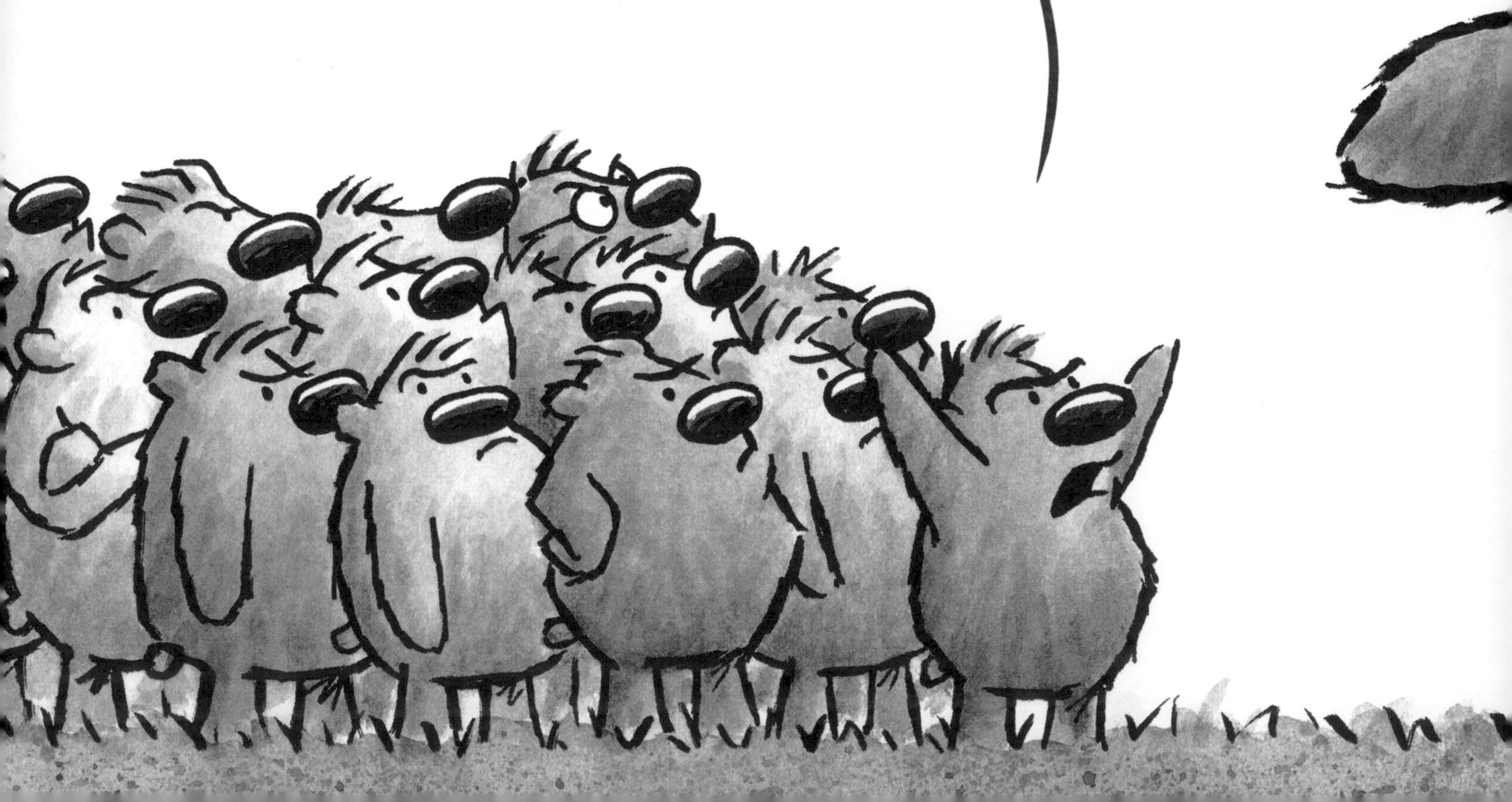

Big!

See? I am *not* small.

No, you are
not big.
You are big
and
you are small.

And you are
not small.
You are small
and
you are big.

You are hairy.